STALKED BY THE DOCTOR

EMMA BRAY

CHAPTER
ONE

Paul

THE FLUORESCENT LIGHTS flicker on as I stride through the emergency room doors. My white coat billows behind me, a symbol of the authority and duty I bear.

"Dr. Jameson, you're late again." Dr. Gerald Thomas fixes me with a stern look, his salt-and-pepper beard bristling.

I shoot him an apologetic glance and continue walking. "My apologies, Dr. Thomas. Traffic was a nightmare."

He huffs in disapproval but says nothing more. I breathe an inward sigh of relief. As head of the hospital, Dr. Thomas expects perfection from his staff. One misstep is all it takes to land in his bad graces.

My colleagues greet me with nods and smiles as I make my rounds. "Morning Dr. Jameson," Nurse Collins says. "We have a full house today."

"As always," I reply, scanning the bustling emergency room. My gaze settles on a young woman sitting alone in the corner, her pale, delicate features etched with a profound sadness. She glances up and our eyes meet, hers a striking grey that reflect a depth of experience belying her youth.

A fierce surge of protectiveness rises in my chest at the sight of her. Who is this girl who seems to have endured such hardship? I yearn to comfort her, to chase the shadows from those depthless eyes. To know what has wounded her so.

"Dr. Jameson?" Nurse Collins prompts, a knowing smile playing at the edge of her mouth. I drag my gaze from the girl, heat creeping up the back of my neck.

Clearing my throat, I turn to Nurse Collins. "What do we have this morning?"

As Nurse Collins briefs me on the day's cases, I steal another glance at the girl. She's watching me too, a faint blush staining her pale cheeks. I wonder if she feels this strange connection between us as intensely as I do. I ache to speak with her, to learn her name.

Who is she? And why has she captivated me so completely?

My cock stiffens as I think of her, desire pooling hot in my groin. I shift discreetly, trying to hide my arousal, but I can't tear my gaze from her.

Who *is* she? I have to know.

I make my way over to her as Nurse Collins calls the next patient. The girl shrinks back into her seat, clutching a worn backpack to her chest, eyes darting around the bustling room.

I stop a few feet away, offering what I hope is a reassuring smile. "Hello. I'm Dr. Jameson."

She blinks up at me, grey eyes wary. "Britney," she says softly. Her voice is like velvet, stroking along my skin.

"It's a pleasure to meet you, Britney." I slide into the seat beside her, heart pounding. This close, I can see faint bruises mottling her pale throat. A flare of anger ignites in my chest at the sight. Who dared to hurt her? "How are you feeling today?"

She shrugs, gaze dropping to her hands. "I'm okay."

I frown, reaching to gently tilt her chin up. She flinches at my touch, and I drop my hand, cursing myself. I've frightened her. The thought of anyone frightening this slip of a girl makes my blood boil.

"You're safe here," I assure her, keeping my voice soft and calm. I want nothing more than to pull her into my arms, to shield her from whatever demons haunt her.

She searches my face, as though looking for any hint of deception. Finally, she nods.

Triumph surges through me. I've gained her trust, if only for a moment. I want more. I want everything she'll give me.

I clear my throat, struggling to focus. "Can you tell me about yourself, Britney? What brings you to the hospital today?"

She worries her lower lip between her teeth, gaze darting away. I resist the urge to reach out and still her restless hands.

"I haven't been feeling well lately," she says at last. "Dizzy spells, fatigue."

I nod, scribbling notes on her chart. "Your blood work shows you're quite anemic. Have you experienced nausea or vomiting as well?"

A faint blush stains her cheeks. She shakes her head.

"I see." I frown, piecing together the clues. Her bruised throat. Her malnourishment. The evasiveness in her gaze.

She's not telling me everything.

"Britney," I say gently. "I'm here to help you. But I can only do that if you're honest with me about what's going on."

Her eyes shine with tears as she looks up at me. In that moment I'm lost. I would move heaven and earth to take away her pain.

"Please tell me," I urge softly. "You can trust me."

She takes a deep breath, steeling herself. When she speaks, her voice is scarcely more than a whisper.

"My stepdad, he—he hurts me sometimes."

A strangled sound leaves my throat as my vision goes red.

"Oh," her cheeks color when she realizes what I think she means by that. "Not like *that*. I mean, I don't like the way he looks at me. He's never t-touched me. I'm still a virgin," she whisper tearfully.

All the blood in my body goes south at her admission. I feel almost dizzy with the knowledge. This beautiful girl is untouched.

Sweet, innocent, *ripe*.

My cock aches to shred that innocence.

"What does he do to hurt you, sweetheart?" I ask her, tyring to keep my mind on her health needs and off the aching flesh in my pants.

"H-he won't let me eat and—he locks me in my room." Her words dissolve into quiet sobs.

Rage bubbles up inside me, white-hot and venomous. The bastard. The filthy, sadistic bastard. I pull Britney into my arms, cradling her as she weeps against my chest.

"Shh," I soothe, stroking her hair. "You're safe now. I won't let anyone hurt you again. I promise."

She's not going back to her stepdad's. That I vow. I'll make sure she has a place to stay.

A fierce protectiveness rises in me as I hold this broken girl in my arms. She is mine now. I will keep her safe.

And I will make her tormentor pay.

———

I ease Britney back onto the bed, tucking the blankets around her.

"Get some rest," I say gently. "I'll be back to check on you soon.

She nods, eyes already drooping shut, exhausted from her ordeal. I watch her for a long moment, tracing the delicate lines of her face. Such innocence. Such vulnerability.

I'm hard as a rock just thinking about it.

With an effort, I turn away and stride out of the room. I have work to do. Plans to make.

Britney's tormentor will not get away with this. I will hunt him down if it's the last thing I do. And when I find him, he will beg for mercy before I rip his pathetic life away.

No one hurts what's mine.

My hands clench into fists, nails biting into my palms. The beast within snarls and strains at its chains, hungry for vengeance. I take a deep breath, regaining control.

I'm a doctor. I'm supposed to ease pain—not create it. But an exception must be made in this case. Only a monster would harm such an innocent creature, and I feel like it's my personal duty to make him pay.

Patience. I must have patience.

When the time is right, I will feed the beast. And it will feast on agony and death.

For now, I return to my rounds, hiding my rage behind a mask of cool professionalism. But my mind is churning, thoughts of Britney and retribution swirling in a relentless loop.

She is mine now. I will keep her safe.

And her tormentor will pay the price in blood.

CHAPTER
TWO

Paul

I'M DRAWN to her room like a moth to flame. My footsteps quicken as I walk down the sterile hallway, eager to see her pale face and wispy blonde hair splayed across the stark white pillow.

"Dr. Jameson." The nurse smiles knowingly, her gaze flickering between me and Room 312.

"Nurse Chen. How is our patient today?" I keep my tone casual, professional. But inside, my heart hammers with anticipation.

"Her condition remains stable. She's awake if you'd like to check on her."

"Thank you, I will."

I knock softly and push open the door. Britney looks up, her gray eyes lighting up when she sees me. A smile teases the corners of her soft lips.

"Dr. Jameson." Her voice is barely above a whisper, but it thrills through me like a shot of morphine.

"Ms. Bailey. How are you feeling today?" I perch on the edge of her bed, reaching to clasp her delicate hand in mine. She doesn't pull away.

"Better, now that you're here." A becoming blush stains her pale cheeks. I find myself stroking the back of her hand with my thumb, unable to stop.

"I'm glad to hear you're improving." The words sound strangled. I clear my throat, shifting in my seat. "Your test results look good. If you continue to heal at this rate, you should be discharged in a few days."

Panic flares in her eyes, and her fingers tighten around mine. "A few days? But...where will I go?"

"Don't worry," I murmur, still stroking my hand across her knuckles. "I'll take care of you."

She searches my face, looking for affirmation. And she'll find it. I won't let her go. Not now, not ever.

She's *mine*.

"Promise?" Her lips tremble.

"Promise." I give her my most reassuring smile. "You can trust me."

And she does.

A smile teases the corners of her soft lips.

"Tell me about yourself," I say gently. "I want to know everything."

Her eyes widen, then drop to our joined hands. "There's not much to tell. My life hasn't been...easy."

"You can tell me anything." I squeeze her hand encouragingly. "Your past is safe with me."

She takes a deep, shuddering breath. "My mother left when I was little. My stepdad..." Her voice trails off, eyes glistening with tears. "He always told me I was lucky he kept me around, that he should throw me out on the street, that I was so pathetic my own mother left me. He hit me," she whispers.

Rage ignites in my chest, white-hot and searing. The urge to hunt down this bastard and end him is nearly overwhelming. I force myself to stay calm, to focus on Britney. She needs me.

"I'm so sorry you went through that," I say softly. "You deserved so much better."

A tear slips down her cheek. I have to figh the urge to brush it away.

"You're perfect." The words are out before I can stop them. Her eyes fly to mine, wide and wondering. "You're special, Britney. You're strong and brave, and you deserve to be happy. I'm going to make sure of that."

"You..." She swallows hard. "You really mean that?"

"With all my heart." I lift her hand and press my lips to her palm, thrilling at her quiet gasp.

"No one's ever cared about me like this before," she whispers.

"Get used to it." I smile down at her, triumph and desire swirling inside me. She's falling, tumbling into my waiting arms.

Soon, she'll be mine forever.

———

I become determined to protect Britney from any harm, feeling a growing obsession with her well-being.

My need to keep Britney safe borders on madness. I think of little else—her fragile smile, the haunted look in her eyes, the scars on her pale skin. Scars *he* put there.

Rage rises in me again, acidic and choking. I have to find him. Have to make him pay for what he's done.

But first, I need to ensure Britney's safety. I study her chart for any signs of complications, check on her at all hours, bristle when other doctors go near her. She is *mine* to care for. *Mine* to protect.

I find out where she's been living with her piece of shit stepdad. They live in a rundown apartment across town, the lobby reeking of stale cigarettes and defeat.

My hands clench into fists, nails biting into my

palms. This is no place for my Britney. She should be cared for, cherished.

I make a decision then. When the time is right, I'll bring her home with me.

For now, I put her up in an apartment near mine.

Where I can keep her close, keep her safe.

Always.

———

When Britney is discharged from the hopsital, she trustingly puts her little hand in mine and watches with wide eyes as I open the door to the apartment I secured her.

"Dr. Jameson!" she gasps. "This is too much! There's no way I can pay you for this."

"You being safe is enough, Britney."

She bites her lip, and I ball my hands into fists to keep from dragging her into my arms and rutting her here and now. "I'm going to get a job," she promises me. "I'll pay you back somehow, I promise.

I finally allow myself to touch her lips. I hold a finger to them, my balls tightening painfully as I feel her warm breath on my skin.

Jesus, the way she's looking up at me. All sweet and innocent.

"Can you be happy here?"

She swallows and nods. "Yes, it's beautiful. More than I ever dreamed of."

I nod back at her. "Then, that's payment enough, Britney."

As much as I yearn to stay longer, I know that doing so will only test my restraint, and it's already at its limits. I certainly don't want Britney thinking she has to pay for her apartment with her body, which is what I'm afraid she'll think if I make a move on her now.

So, I leave. It almost kills me to leave her, but I know she'll be fine.

I've made sure of it with all the cameras I had put in her apartment.

———

I've become *obsessed*. In between hospital shifts, I track Britney's movements—the coffee shop where she works, the laundromat she frequents, the park where she sits alone on a wooden bench, gazing out at a pond filled with ducks.

She interacts with few people, speaks to no one beyond casual pleasantries. I shouldn't take pleasure in this, but I do. I want to be the only light in her world.

I got her a cell phone, and I love see her face light up when she gets a text from me.

My sweet, precious girl.

I learn her schedule, the patterns of her days. And I look for any threats, any danger. Especially *men*. A few try to flirt with her, buy her drinks or ask for her number.

Their interest in her enrages me. I want to stride right up to them, snarl that she belongs to *me*. But I restrain myself.

For now.

When the time is right, Britney will be mine. No other man will so much as look at her again.

And anyone who dares try will suffer the consequences.

Fueled by my obsession and desire to keep Britney safe, I track down Britney's stepdad and kill him, ensuring he can never hurt her again.

It takes days of watching and waiting, but I finally spot him—a hulking brute of a man stumbling out of a dive bar, reeking of cheap whiskey and stale cigarettes.

My hands clench into fists as I think of him laying a single finger on Britney. The rage bubbles up inside me, hot and venomous, clouding my vision with a red haze.

I follow him into a dimly lit alleyway, my steps silent on the cracked concrete. When he turns to take a piss against the wall, I strike.

A sharp blow to the back of his skull sends him

crashing to his knees. Before he can cry out, I loop a cord around his throat and pull tight, cutting off his airway.

He struggles against me, clawing at the cord and gasping for breath, but I hold on with a strength borne of madness. "You will never touch her again," I hiss into his ear.

When his body goes limp, I release my hold and let him drop to the ground. I stand over him, chest heaving, staring at his lifeless form. A grim satisfaction settles in my gut. Britney is safe now. Protected. By *me*.

I meticulously cover my tracks, moving the body to an abandoned warehouse and arranging it to appear like just another drunk who died in his vomit. No one will look too closely at the ligature marks on his neck or question how he ended up in this place.

After cleaning myself up, I head over to Britney's apartment and check in on her. She smiles when she sees me, a warmth flooding her pale eyes.

"You always make me feel better," she says softly.

I reach out and brush a strand of hair from her face, my touch lingering. "I will always keep you safe," I vow.

And she has no idea of the lengths I will go to in order fulfill that promise.

Despite the darkness of my actions, I feel a sense of relief and satisfaction. I've never killed a man. Vowed to never do no harm. But I did what was necessary to protect Britney.

The rage that consumed me during the act has faded, leaving behind a profound calm. I examine myself for any signs of regret or guilt but find none. Killing him was the only way to ensure Britney's safety and well-being. She is too precious, too vulnerable, to be subjected to monsters like him any longer.

I think of her bruised and broken body, the haunted look in her eyes, and my hands clench into fists. No, I did the right thing. The only thing. Britney is mine to protect now.

I continue to visit Britney, maintaining a facade of professionalism while secretly reveling in our connection.

"You're looking brighter today," I say, smiling down at Britney. She smiles back, a flush staining her pale cheeks. I reach out to take her hand in mine, stroking my thumb over her knuckles.

"I'm feeling better," she says. "Stronger. Thanks to you."

"I'm glad to hear that." I give her hand a gentle squeeze. "You deserve to feel safe and happy."

Her eyes shine with tears as she looks up at me. "What would I do without you?"

A fierce possessiveness rises in my chest, and I have to fight the urge to crush her in my arms. Instead, I school my features into a mask of professional concern.

"You don't have to worry about that," I say. "I will always be here for you."

She doesn't realize the truth in my words. I will never leave her side now. She belongs to me, just as I belong to her, and not even death will keep us apart.

She gazes up at me with tears glistening in her eyes. "You've been here for me when no one else was. You're the only one I can trust." Her fingers tighten around mine, clinging to me like I'm her only lifeline in a churning sea.

A fierce surge of possessiveness rises in my chest, and I squeeze her hand in return. "You can always trust me," I say, staring into her eyes. "I will never leave you, Britney. *Never*."

She smiles then, soft and serene, leaning back against the couch. The tension seems to seep from her body as she relaxes into sleep, still holding fast to my hand.

I remain seated beside her, watching the steady rise and fall of her chest.

I don't know how long I watch her. I could sit here forever watching my angel sleep.

Britney's eyes flutter open and she smiles up at me, sleepy and unguarded. "You're still here," she murmurs.

"Where else would I be?" I ask, brushing a lock of hair from her forehead.

She catches my hand, pressing a soft kiss to my palm. My heart clenches at the simple gesture, heat pooling low in my belly. I want nothing more than to crush her to me, feel the warmth of her body against mine as I claim what is rightfully mine.

But I restrain myself, keeping my touches light and professional. There will be time enough for intimacy. For now, I am content simply being by her side, watching over her as she sleeps.

CHAPTER
THREE

Britney

THE MARBLE FLOORS *shine under my bare feet as I pad into the kitchen, the chill seeping into my bones. I run my fingers along the sleek countertops, still not quite believing this luxury apartment is mine.*

After years of living in squalor, Dr. Jameson rescued me. He swept in like my savior and rescued me from the monster who made my life a living hell. Now I live here, safe within these walls of wealth, my body and mind finally at peace.

I owe him everything. My life, my freedom, my safety. He is the reason I can breathe without fear, sleep without nightmares, and walk without watching over my shoulder.

The intercom buzzes, pulling me from my thoughts. I

rush to answer, heart pounding. "Dr. Jameson, you're early."

His chuckle comes through, deep and throaty. "I couldn't wait to see you. Are you ready for your checkup?"

Heat floods my cheeks at the thought of his hands on my body. "Yes, come on up."

I pace the foyer, smoothing my clothes and hair until the knock sounds. When I open the door, his scent of sandalwood and antiseptic washes over me.

Dr. Jameson steps inside, tall and broad shouldered in his white coat. His eyes gleam behind wire-rimmed glasses as he looks me over. "You're looking well. How have you been settling in?"

"Wonderfully, thanks to you." I grasp his hands, pulse racing at the warmth and strength in them. "You've given me a new life, and I'll never be able to repay you."

He squeezes my hands, the gesture somehow both comforting and stirring. "Seeing you safe and happy is repayment enough." His gaze turns molten, and a shiver runs through me. "Now, let's get started with your checkup, shall we?"

Heat pools low in my belly at the promise in his words.

I lead him to the bedroom, heart pounding. He closes the door behind us with a soft click, and I perch on the edge of the bed.

Dr. Jameson washes his hands in the en suite bathroom.

"Remove your shirt and bra, please, so I can listen to your heart and lungs."

My fingers tremble as I obey, baring my chest to his gaze. He turns, eyes darkening at the sight of me, and strides over with his stethoscope.

"Deep breaths," he murmurs, and places the cold metal disc against my skin. His touch ignites my nerves, and I struggle to inhale and exhale steadily.

He moves the stethoscope across my chest, lingering over my breasts. A soft groan escapes him, and heat pools between my thighs.

Finally, he straightens, clearing his throat. "Your heart and lungs sound strong and healthy." His gaze rakes over me, simmering with desire. "You seem to be in peak physical and mental condition. However, I should perform a...more thorough examination, to be safe."

My lips part on a gasp as understanding hits me. "Yes, Dr. Jameson. Please examine me...completely."

A predatory smile curves his mouth. "Lie back on the bed and remove the rest of your clothes. This will be a very hands-on examination."

Shivering in anticipation, I lie back and strip off my pants and panties. I watch through hooded eyes as he undresses, desire burning hotter with every inch of skin he reveals.

He looms over me, gloriously naked, eyes glowing with

hunger. "What a perfect specimen you are," he purrs. "This examination will be most...pleasurable."

He lowers himself onto me, and I moan as our bodies align in delicious friction. At last, my salvation is at hand.

I arch into him as he thrusts inside me, stretching and filling me. Our cries of pleasure mingle and echo off the walls.

With each drive of his hips, the ache in my core intensifies. The friction borders on pain, but I crave more. Harder, faster, deeper.

He obliges, pinning my wrists above my head and snapping his hips against me. I'm drowning in sensation, losing myself in the rhythm of our joining.

Nothing exists but this moment, this pleasure, this connection.

Dr. Jameson groans, his thrusts becoming erratic. "So perfect, so tight. You're mine, all mine."

His words trigger a rush of heat and I shatter around him, back arching in ecstasy. He finds his own release with a shout, spilling inside me.

We lie together, limbs entwined, breathing hard. I curl into his side, basking in the afterglow.

I awaken with a gasp, my body slick with sweat and my core throbbing. I slide my hand between my legs and groan at the wetness I find there.

Guilt and shame flood me. The things I dream about Dr. Jameson are wrong. I'm his patient.

But still, I can't help but think of the handsome doctor. His kind eyes, the way I wish he would do the things to me I dream about.

I toss and turn all night, wrestling with my conflicting emotions.

And then I drift off to sleep again...

Dr. Jameson arrives for my appointment. I meet his gaze steadily, ignoring the rush of heat at seeing him again. "We can't do this anymore. I think it's best if you transfer me to another doctor."

His eyes flash with anger and something darker. "I won't allow it."

I swallow hard, unnerved by his tone. "I'm your patient, not your possession. You have no right to tell me what I can and can't do regarding my own care."

He stalks toward me, and I back up instinctively. He crowds me against the wall, hands braced on either side of my head, and leans in until our noses nearly touch. "You belong to me now, Britney. I won't give you up so easily."

Panic rises in my chest at his words, yet there's also a thrill at the thought that he wants to possess, that I drive him to such madness. I try to push him away, but he doesn't budge. "Let me go! I never want to see you again."

"You don't get to make that choice." His eyes are smoldering. "You're mine, and I always get what's mine."

He claims my mouth in a bruising kiss, and I renew my struggles, terror and desire flooding my senses. But he's too strong, and I'm helpless in his grip. As darkness overtakes me, his sinister promise echoes in my mind.

I belong to him now.

I come to with a gasp, disoriented and confused. It takes me a moment to realize I'm in my apartment, safe in my own bed.

Just a nightmare. Well, can I call it a nightmare if I half liked it? But what the hell is wrong with me that I even like the thought of Dr. Jameson giving me no choice? The memory of Dr. Jameson's possessive grip and chilling words still haunt me and make my sex damp. I press my thighs together to try to ease the ache that blossoms there.

When Dr. Jameson arrives for my appointment later, I have to focus on breathing steadily so he doesn't pick up on the erratic beating of my heart. I stare at a spot on the wall, avoiding his gaze, afraid he'll see right through me.

"You seem distracted today," he observes. "Is everything alright?"

I nod mutely, biting my tongue to avoid blurting out what's really on my mind. *I want you so bad I dream bad things about you.*

"I worry about you, Britney," he continues, misinterpreting my silence. "You've been through so much, and I just want you to know I'm here for you if there's anything you need to get off your chest."

His concern makes my stomach turn. He's so good, so kind. He'd probably run for the hills if he knew the sick thoughts I have about him. How I want him to possess me, to control me.

I swallow and nod, unable to speak.

When he leans down to listen to my heartbeat, his breath feathers across my neck, and I stiffen. His scent envelops me, and desire moistens my panties.

He pulls back to study me, and I avoid meeting his gaze, afraid he'll see the truth reflected there. But then his fingers curl under my chin, forcing my eyes to his.

"You know I'm here for you, don't you?"

"Yes, Dr. Jameson," I make myself whisper. "I'm just tired."

He looks like he might say more, but then he simply nods and takes his leave.

And I'm left alone with my aching pussy and lustful thoughts.

Maybe I am a whore, just like my stepdad always said I would be.

Paul

THE SUMMONS ARRIVES during my morning rounds. A clipped note in Dr. Thomas's precise hand instructs me to report to his office immediately.

My heart sinks. Whatever this is about, it won't be good. Dr. Thomas tolerates no infractions, no missteps. Perfection is the only acceptable standard.

I finish with my last patient and head to the executive wing, a twisting serpent of corridors lined with antique oak panels and oil portraits of venerable hospital patrons. The scent of lemon polish and money lingers here, a world away from the chemical cacophony of the wards.

At last I reach the double doors of Dr. Thomas's office, steeling myself before entering. He looks up from a stack of papers, pale eyes peering at me over the rim of his glasses.

"Dr. Jameson. Thank you for coming." His tone is cordial, but there's an edge to it. A razor-sharp warning. "Please, have a seat."

I sink into one of the leather chairs facing his massive oak desk, pulse racing. *Stay calm. You've done nothing wrong.*

I almost snort at myself. I know exactly what I've been doing. Lusting after my young patient. I'm a sick bastard.

"I've noticed you've been making a number of house calls recently." Dr. Thomas leans back in his chair, steepling his fingers. "Far more than usual. Might I ask what's prompted this change in your routine?"

"Just following up with a few patients to monitor their recovery." Even to my own ears, the excuse sounds weak.

"Really." He arches an eyebrow. "Because from what I can tell, you seem to be making frequent visits to only one patient. A Miss Britney Bailey, if I'm not mistaken."

My mouth goes dry. He knows.

"I'm waiting for an explanation, Dr. Jameson." His eyes gleam behind those wire-rimmed spectacles, a predator circling his prey. "And it had better be good."

I grasp for words, coming up empty. There is no explanation, no excuse that can justify my actions. Nothing but the truth—that I've thrown away my ethics and risked my career for my sick obsession.

Dr. Thomas's lips thin into a disapproving line. "As I suspected. I'm disappointed, Paul. Fraternizing with patients is unacceptable. You know that."

"I know," I say weakly.

"Yet here we are." He shakes his head. "You're a talented doctor, but you seem determined to sabotage yourself at every turn. This obsession of yours has clouded your judgment and compromised your integrity as a physician."

Each word strikes like a blow. He's not wrong. I've betrayed the oath I took to do no harm. All for the sake of desire.

"I'm prepared to overlook this incident," Dr. Thomas says, "if you agree to end your relationship with Miss Bailey immediately and refocus your efforts on your work. But if I catch you fraternizing with patients again, I will have no choice but to take disciplinary action. Do you understand?"

His ultimatum rings in my ears, echoing the death knell of my hopes and dreams. I know what I should do, what any reasonable person would do. Walk away from Britney before I cause her—or myself—any more harm.

But how can I give her up? After everything we've shared, the thought of losing her is unbearable. I'm torn between my duty as a doctor and the longing of my heart, trapped between an impossible choice.

Dr. Thomas's eyes narrow, waiting for my response. The silence stretches, tension crackling in the air as I grapple for an answer.

Finally, I meet his gaze, jaw clenched. "I understand."

The words taste bitter on my tongue, but they're enough to satisfy him. He nods, leaning back in his chair once more.

"Very good. I trust this unpleasantness will be behind us, then." His tone brokers no argument. "You're dismissed."

I stand stiffly and make my way to the door, anger and despair churning inside me. I

I stalk down the hospital corridor, fists clenched at my sides. How dare he interfere in my personal life? What business is it of his who I see outside of work?

Yet try as I might, I can't ignore the voice of reason in my head. He's right—my relationship with Britney is completely unethical. As her doctor, I have a responsibility to put her wellbeing first. If our secret relationship came to light, it could destroy her already fragile trust.

Guilt washes over me in a sickening wave. What

was I thinking, preying on her vulnerability like that? She's barely more than a child, struggling to find her way in the world, and I took advantage of her in a moment of weakness.

The memory of her soft skin against mine fills me with equal parts shame and desire. I'm disgusted with myself, but I can't stop craving her with an intensity that steals my breath away.

By the time I reach the staff parking lot, my hands have stopped shaking, but my mind is still in turmoil. I know what I have to do, however much it may pain me. As soon as I get home, I'll call Britney and end this once and for all before it spirals even further out of control.

It's the only way to absolve my conscience and protect her from any more harm.

———

I pace the length of my apartment, fingers combing through my hair as I struggle for the right words.

With a heavy sigh, I pick up the phone and dial Britney's number before I can change my mind. She answers on the second ring, her voice soft and breathless. "Dr. Jameson?"

A bolt of longing spears through me at the sound of her voice. I squeeze my eyes shut, gripping the phone hard enough to ache. "Britney, we need to talk."

Silence.

I swallow against the lump in my throat. I can't do it. God help me, but I can't do it. The words stick in my throat, choking me. I can't do this. I can't give her up, not for Dr. Thomas or anyone else. There has to be another way, some way to throw him off the scent and keep her safe. "I was wondering if you'd like to have dinner with me tonight."

I can hear the smile in her voice as she answers back enthusiastically, "I'd love that!"

My heart warms. "I'll come right over to pick you up. You mind if I bring you back to my place and we eat in?"

"That sounds great," she adds with an adorable little girl quality to her voice that has my hands flexing. This is dangerous. Oh, so dangerous. I shouldn't bring her here to my place.

But it's like I'm on a fast-traveling train, and there's no brakes. I can't stop this—no matter how hard I try.

Dr. Thomas be damned. No one will ever take her from me.

FIVE

Paul

"YOU READY?" I ask Britney, my mouth dry as I extend the invitation. She looks up at me with those wide, gray eyes, a blush crossing her delicate features.

"Yes," she says softly. My heart leaps at her words.

I usher her into my sleek black sedan, her scent enveloping me as she slides into the seat beside me. I clench the steering wheel to stop myself from reaching for her, my knuckles turning white with the effort.

We make light conversation on the drive to my house, a modern architectural masterpiece perched on the outskirts of the city. I lead her up the winding path to my front door, hyperaware of how close she walks beside me.

Over dinner, I maintain a veneer of professionalism. But it's a constant struggle not to stare at the graceful line of her neck as she eats, not to reach out and caress the soft curve of her cheek. I yearn to possess her, body and soul.

"The food is delicious," she says, her eyes meeting mine for a fleeting moment.

"I'm glad you're enjoying it," I say evenly. My restraint is hanging by a thread as sharp as a scalpel's edge.

We continue our desultory conversation, but the tension is almost palpable. Every word, every gesture is layered with hidden meaning.

After dinner, I escort Britney back to her apartment, ensuring her safety and maintaining a respectful distance.

The chill night air does little to cool my fevered thoughts, though. I can still taste Britney on my lips, feel the warmth of her body pressed against mine.

At her apartment door, she turns to me. "Thank you for dinner. I had a lovely time."

"The pleasure was mine." I take her hand and brush my lips across her knuckles, watching her pupils dilate. "Sleep well, Britney."

I wait until she's safely inside before I return to my

car, my strides fueled by restless energy. The beast within me is stirring, clawing to break free of its chains. I hurry home, intent on my mission.

Back in my study, I activate the hidden cameras. Britney moves through the range of the lenses, a goddess in my private heaven.

She kicks off her heels and stretches like a cat, revealing a strip of smooth skin above her skirt. I groan, heat pooling in my abdomen.

When she undresses for bed, I catch a glimpse of lace and silk undergarments in dove gray, the color of her eyes. The thought sends a spear of lust through me.

Britney slips between the sheets, her golden hair fanning across the pillow.

Finally, I can stand it no longer. I jerk my cock free of my pants and imagine...

I pull her into my arms and crush my lips against hers. She opens her mouth with a soft sigh, her hands twining in my hair.

Our kiss deepens, fueled by months of pent-up desire. I back her against the wall, pinning her in place. She moans, the sound vibrating against my lips. I can no longer tell where she ends and I begin. We are two souls fused into one.

I break away, breathless. Britney looks up at me, her eyes dark with longing.

"Call me Paul," I whisper.

"Paul," she echoes, and my name on her lips sounds sweeter than any symphony.

Our fate is sealed. She is mine, now and forever.

"Fuck, baby. Do you know how long I've wanted to get inside this pretty little fuck hole? Bet that little virgin cunt is dripping for me, isn't it?"

She moans. "I've been saving it all for you, Paul. All for you."

I fall to my knees, her pussy coming into view.

And then I nut. I can never get past the imagined image of her pussy without coming. Jesus, if I can't even imagine her young cunt without coming, I don't know how I'd ever even get it inside her without busting.

I hold my messy cock in my hand and stare at her on the screen. Her pink lips are parted in sleep. She looks so cherubic.

So mother*fucking* innocent.

This girl will be the death of me.

———

The next evening, I'm on my way to Britney's when a flash of movement catches my eye on the camera feed I have pulled up on my phone. A figure has entered the frame of Camera Three, the lobby of Britney's apartment. It's a man in a leather jacket, tall and athletic.

Britney emerges from the hallway, looking adorable in an oversized sweater and leggings. The sight of her makes my blood boil. The man's gaze instantly snaps to her, and he starts making is way over to her.

Of course. What man in his right mind wouldn't notice her?

I grip the phone in my hand so hard I'm surprised I don't shatter the screen. She's *mine, all mine*! Who gave this intruder the right to stand there devouring her with his eyes?

"Hey, gorgeous," the audacious young man purrs.

Britney looks up at him, startled.

That man reaches out and tucks a lock of hair behind Britney's ear. "Where you heading, hot stuff?"

Rage sears through my veins like acid. How dare he touch her? I'll rip his hands off before he can lay another finger on her.

Britney steps back from him, her eyes wide with shock. "Um, nowhere." She's so innocent, she's completely caught off guard by his attention.

Don't worry, Britney, baby. I'm coming for you.

This fucker will pay for his insolence.

I burst into the lobby, chest heaving, fists clenched. I've worked myself into a fury.

"Dr. Jameson?" Britney's eyes widen when she sees me, and then they settle into relief. "What are you doing here?"

I don't answer her. Instead, I approach the fucker who dared to touch what's *mine*.

I tower over him, pushing my face in his. "Listen, asshat. You don't touch her again. And if I ever see you near her again, you'd better believe you'll be eating these fists."

The punk backs away with a look of terror on his face, and I turn to Britney. She's watching me with shocked eyes.

"Let's go," I say gruffly, reaching out for her hand and leading her back to her apartment.

We walk back to her place in silence but for the faint strains of a symphony coming from the lobby.

"Dr. Jameson, you're scaring me."

Scaring her. The words cut through my rage, leaving me stunned. I release her at once, horrified by my actions. What have I done?

Britney stumbles back, looking up at me dubiously. "Dr. Jameson," she begins again.

"Paul," I rasp out. "Call me Paul. *Please*."

"Paul," Britney whispers so softly I almost don't hear her.

But it's enough. God help me, it's enough.

I fucking lose it. With a groan, I haul the girl of my dreams into my arms and crash my lips down on hers.

I devour her at first, but then she begins to kiss me

back, and I'm shocked, my kiss slowing down in wonder.

Our lips move in a slow, sensual rhythm. Her mouth is soft and pliant under mine, her tongue shyly seeking mine. Heat coils in my belly, spreading lower. *Perfect girl. Beautiful, perfect girl.* My hands slide down to grip her waist, pulling her closer. She sighs into the kiss, her fingers tightening in my hair.

I could kiss her forever. When we finally break apart, we're both breathing hard. Her cheeks are flushed, her lips kiss-swollen. She looks up at me through lowered lashes, gray eyes dark with desire.

"Paul," she whispers. My name on her lips is a caress. No one has ever said it like that.

"Fuck, Britney." My voice is rough with longing.

There's too much space between us. I pull her into my arms, holding her close. Her head rests over my heart, her hair soft against my chin.

After a long moment, she draws back to gaze up at me.

I brush a lock of hair from her eyes, tracing the curve of her cheek.

Still, we don't speak.

We stand there together, wrapped in each other's arms, as shadows lengthen across the floor. Tomorrow there will be complications to consider, obstacles to overcome. But for now, it's enough just to hold her. To know that she's *mine*, the way I have always been hers.

I know, with a bone-deep certainty, that I will never let her go. No matter what it takes, Britney Bailey belongs with *me*.

So, I finally stop fighting it and kiss her again.

CHAPTER
SIX

Britney

PAUL KISSES ME AGAIN, his lips branding my skin as he backs me into my apartment, the door slamming behind us.

"I want you. *Now*." His voice is rough with desire.

My heart pounds. I know this is wrong, that he's my doctor, but I can't resist him. I don't want to.

"Then take me," I whisper.

Paul makes a strangled sound as he takes my hand and leads me to the bedroom, our fingers intertwined, our bodies already craving each other.

The room is dimly lit by the streetlights outside.

Paul turns to face me, his eyes dark with lust. "Once we do this, you're mine, Britney."

A thrill runs through me at his commanding tone. All that can be heard is our ragged breathing, and then I pull my shirt over my head, my nipples hardening in the cool air. Paul unbuckles his belt, his gaze fixed on me, watching my every move.

I slide my jeans down my legs, kicking them aside. I'm shy. I've never been naked before a man before, but I force myself to not hide. The way Paul's hungry gaze devours me gives me courage.

Paul shrugs off his shirt, revealing his toned torso. The bulge in his boxers leaves nothing to the imagination. I feel a moment of worry when I see how huge that outline is.

And I don't know what I'm doing, but I follow some instinct I have to *taste* him. I sink to my knees, anticipation pulsing through my veins. I pull down his boxers, his erection springing free, hard and thick.

Paul hisses out a breath when I wrap my hands around his thick length.

And then I take him in my mouth, inch by inch, until he hits the back of my throat. Paul lets out a guttural moan, grabbing my hair.

"Oh, fuck. Just like that, baby. Take it all. Fuck, Britney, are you trying to kill me?"

I move back and forth, my tongue swirling around

his length. The sounds of my sucking fill the room, punctuated by Paul's ragged breathing.

I feel powerful, and I feel my folds slickening, Paul's groans spurring me on.

"Fuck, Britney. So good. You're mine now, all fucking mine." Paul's words send a thrill through me. Yes, I'm his, and his alone. There's no going back now.

Paul finally pulls me up by my hair and crushes his mouth against mine, tasting himself on my lips. Our bodies press together, skin on skin, and I know this is only the beginning. The beginning of Paul's possession over me, body and soul, and I welcome it. I welcome all of it.

Paul lays me back on the bed, his eyes dark with lust.

"I'm going to ruin you for any other man."

With that promise, he captures my mouth again, his kiss bruising and demanding. I arch into him, craving his touch, his possession.

Paul's hands roam over my body, kneading my breasts before moving lower. He slides two fingers inside me, stroking my inner walls. I gasp into his mouth, pleasure rippling through me.

"So wet for me already," Paul murmurs. "You're mine to do with as I please."

He withdraws his fingers and brings them to my mouth. "Taste yourself."

I suck his fingers clean without hesitation. Paul growls in approval, his pupils dilating and his nostrils flaring.

"Fuck, Britney. Fuck. Got to have you. *Now.*"

My body trembles in anticipation. Paul moves on top of me, gripping my hips. The head of his cock teases my entrance, already slick with my arousal.

"Britney," Paul moans. "Fuck, you have no idea how long I've wanted this baby girl."

"Please," I whisper. "Please, Paul."

He enters me in one swift stroke, filling and stretching me. I cry out, the mix of pain and pleasure intoxicating.

"Oh, sweet Jesus. So tight. So tight! Come on, baby. Don't tighten up on me. Let me in sweetheart, and I'll make it all better. I promise." Paul continues to spew filth in my ear as he keeps pulling back and pushing forward, making his way deeper into me inch by inch.

And when he finally gets all the way he in, he shouts a savage sound before he sets a brutal pace, pounding into me. I meet each thrust, pushing back against him, craving more. Harder, faster, rougher.

Paul obliges, fucking me into the mattress. His fingers dig into my hips, claiming me, possessing me, his for the taking.

Paul and I move together, our bodies in perfect sync. He pounds into me, each stroke more powerful than the last. My orgasm builds within me and I can see the same pleasure on his face.

I come apart beneath him with a scream, my inner walls clenching around his cock as I let go of all my inhibitions. Paul follows soon after, spilling inside me, his warmth flooding my senses as he grunts his release.

We collapse onto the bed, our harsh breathing filling the silence. Paul pulls me against his chest, his heart thudding in time with mine.

We lay spooning afterwards, neither of us able to form proper words quite yet. Paul's hands caress every curve and dip of mine, as if memorizing them for next time. His breath tickles my ear, and I can feel him smiling against my skin.

"You're mine now," he whispers, and I can't help but agree with him. Because he is my world. All that exists is him and me entwined together in a passionate embrace.

Our slick bodies press together, the lingering heat of our passion keeping the chill at bay.

I trace idle patterns across his chest, exploring the plains and valleys of his skin. A contented sigh escapes my lips.

Never in my wildest dreams did I imagine it could be like this. The raw intensity, the intimacy, the bone-deep pleasure that shook me to my core.

Paul tilts my chin up, gazing into my eyes. "Are you all right?" His voice is gruff with concern.

I nod, a blush staining my cheeks. "I didn't know it could be that way. You were...it was..." I falter, at a loss for words.

Paul's gaze grows serious. "Did I hurt you?"

"No," I say. "I mean, it stung a little at first, but then..." I shrug, unsure how to put the rest into words.

Paul's eyes darken with desire. "Then the pleasure took over," he finishes for me. "And now you crave more."

Heat pools low in my belly at his words. My body already awakens for his touch, eager to explore new heights of ecstasy.

Paul rolls on top of me, pinning me beneath him. I gasp as his hardness presses against my thigh.

"Round two?" he asks, his voice a husky promise.

I capture his mouth in a searing kiss, my answer clear. Paul enters me again, slower this time, savoring each inch.

Our lovemaking is tender yet passionate, a dance between two lovers lost in the rhythm of desire.

Paul takes me to the edge and holds me there, his thrusts measured, his eyes burning into mine. "Come for me, Britney," he rasps. "Let go."

His words shatter my control. I come apart with a

cry, clinging to him as waves of pleasure engulf my senses.

Paul follows soon after, his warmth filling me, our hearts beating as one.

We lie in silence, drifting in the peaceful aftermath of our passion. A single thought surfaces in my mind, crystal clear and undeniable.

I'm in love with Paul Jameson.

I think I always have been.

CHAPTER
SEVEN

Paul

THE COLD LINOLEUM floor echoes under my shoes as I stride through the hospital doors. My pulse quickens—whether from the bitter chill outside or the confrontation ahead, I can't tell.

Should I avoid him? No, that will only make things worse. I have to face this head-on.

But if he knows the truth...my career, my reputation—everything I've worked for—will be ruined.

I round the corner and there he is, clipboard in hand, brow creased in concentration. Our eyes meet for a split second before he looks away, jaw clenching.

Shit. He knows.

My mouth goes dry as he approaches, footsteps echoing ominously. I brace myself, clutching my coffee cup like a shield.

"Dr. Jameson." Dr. Thomas's tone is clipped, harsh. "A word, please."

I nod, following him into an empty examination room. The door clicks shut behind us.

He tosses a stack of photos onto his desk. "Explain."

I glance at the top photo: Britney and I walking down the street, arms linked, gazing at each other. The sight fills me with warmth even now.

I meet Thomas's eyes steadily. "I don't owe you any explanations about my personal life."

"You do when it threatens the reputation of my hospital!" He slams a fist onto the desk, eyes blazing. "How dare you carry on with a patient? A vulnerable young girl, no less. Have you no shame?"

"Our relationship is between consenting adults," I say. "Britney is perfectly capable of making her own decisions. I will not apologize for caring about her, nor will I allow you to pass judgment on our relationship."

"Then you leave me no choice." He picks up the phone, punching in numbers with more force than necessary. "The medical board will hear about your unethical behavior. Your career will be over before you can blink."

My blood pounds in my ears, rage and defiance rising in equal measure. Anger flares in my chest, burning away my fear. "My behavior? My private life has nothing to do with my work here."

"It has everything to do with it!" He's nearly shouting now, face beet red. "Your little... dalliance...could cost us our reputation. Our funding. Everything." He takes a menacing step closer. "End it. *Now*. Or I will make sure you never work in this field again."

I stare him down, unflinching. "I will not choose between the woman I love and my career. Do what you have to do."

His lips press into a thin line. "You'll regret this."

The door slams behind me as I stalk away down the hall, pulse pounding in my ears. He can threaten me all he wants. He will not control me.

I storm out of the hospital, pulse racing as I climb into my car. How dare Thomas threaten me like that? As if he has any right to dictate who I can and can't care for. My relationship with Britney is no one's business but our own.

Still, anxiety gnaws at my gut as I drive to Britney's house. Thomas wasn't bluffing about contacting the medical board, and if they decide to investigate, it could mean the end of my career. But I can't give Britney up. I won't. There has to be a way around this, some loophole that will allow us to be together without sacrificing everything I've worked for.

Britney answers the door in a pink bathrobe, hair damp and skin flushed from a shower. Just the sight of her calms my frayed nerves. "You look stressed," she says, forehead creasing with concern. "Did something happen at the hospital?"

I pull her into my arms, breathing in the sweet scent of her shampoo.

Beautiful, precious girl. She's worth a thousand careers.

I pull her into her apartment, kicking the door shut behind us. Thomas may be threatening to destroy me, but right now, with Britney in my arms, it hardly seems to matter. He can expose us, fire me, blacklist me from every hospital in the country—but he will never control me. Not when being with Britney makes me feel so profoundly, dangerously alive.

Our kiss is hungry, devouring, full of teeth and heat. I press her back against the wall, hands roaming as she tugs at my hair. Perhaps this is reckless, perhaps it will end in disaster—but if loving Britney is wrong, then I don't want to be right.

Britney pulls back from me and places a hand on my chest. "Paul, what's wrong?"

Fuck, she can sense it. I sigh, running a hand through my hair.

"The medical director at the hospital knows about us," I admit, the words tumbling out before I can stop them. "He's threatening to have me fired if I don't end our relationship."

Britney's eyes widen, her lips parting in shock. "But he can't do that, can he? I'm eighteen, and you haven't done anything wrong."

"Technically I have, according to the hospital's policy on relationships between staff members and patients." I rake a hand through my hair, pulse pounding at the memory of Thomas's smug expression. "But I don't care about the rules, or my job, or any of it. I only care about you."

"Paul, stop." Britney grasps my face between her hands, gaze intense. "You worked too hard to get where you are today. You can't throw it all away for my sake."

"Watch me," I growl, covering her hands with my own. "I'm not losing you, Britney. Not for Thomas, not for anyone. We'll find another way around this, go somewhere he can't reach us. We'll make it work, I promise you that."

"You're not thinking straight." Britney shakes her head, though her eyes shine with tears. "Your job is your life's work. You can't sacrifice your career for a relationship that might not even last."

Anger flares in my chest at her words. After everything we've shared, how can she doubt my commitment to her? "Don't you understand? There is no life, no future I want if you're not part of it. I love you, Britney, and nothing Thomas does or says will ever change that."

"Paul, please listen to me—"

I crush my mouth against hers, kissing her with a desperation that steals her breath. She hesitates for a single heartbeat before melting into my embrace, her fingers twisting in my hair. We stumble backwards into the bedroom, clothes dropping to the floor between searing kisses and caresses.

I make love to her in a frenzy, trying to convince her without words that I need her more than I need air to breathe. I pound at her savagely like I'm trying to fuck some sense into her until she comes with a high-pitched scream, and I come with a roar, her tight cunt fluttering around me and milking me for all I'm worth.

When at last we lie spent in each other's arms, I know with bone-deep certainty that Britney is my destiny. Thomas and his threats no longer matter. Our future is ours alone to decide.

I cradle Britney close, her head pillowed on my chest as she sleeps. My mind replays the confrontation with Thomas, his fury and threats still ringing in my ears. But in this quiet moment, wrapped in Britney's warmth, the fear and anger fade away.

There is no power on earth that could make me give her up. Our love is worth fighting for, no matter the cost.

CHAPTER
EIGHT

Britney

I SIT ALONE in my apartment, trembling. The heaviness in my chest threatens to crush me.

Tears streak down my face as I stare at the wall, thoughts of Dr. Jameson losing his job echoing in my mind.

Either end it with Paul, or he gets fired. Has his career ruined. Everything he's worked for destroyed.

All because of *me*.

I glance down at my hands, clenching and unclenching. They shake uncontrollably, like the rest of me. Like my world.

Shit. What am I going to do?

Paul loves his job. It's his life, his passion. He saves lives. His work is *important*. I can't be the reason he loses that. I can't ruin him like that.

But God, losing him will kill me.

The thought makes the ache in my chest flare into a physical pain. I press my palm against it, as if that could contain the anguish threatening to consume me.

I love Paul with everything in me. Every broken, battered piece of my soul belongs to him. The thought of walking away from him rips me into shreds.

But I have to. For his sake. Even if it destroys me.

The tears come harder now, wracking sobs tearing from my throat. I bury my face in my hands, curling in on myself.

How did it come to this? All we wanted was to love each other. Why does that have to be wrong?

I know what I have to do. No matter how much it hurts. No matter if it breaks me beyond repair.

Paul's career, his future, his happiness—that's all that matters now. Even if it means losing the only good thing I've ever known.

The only man who was able to reach the dark, hidden places inside me and fill them with light. The only person who has ever seen me.

I take a shuddering breath and steel myself, wiping the tears from my cheeks.

It's time to do what needs to be done. To give Paul

up. It's the only way I can truly love him the way he deserves.

The way I always have.

With all of my broken heart.

I close my eyes, remembering the warmth of Paul's embrace. The safety I felt in his arms. The way he looked at me like I was the sun, the stars, his entire world.

A tear slips free as flashes of our time together assault me.

The night we stayed up late, curled on the couch, talking for hours about everything and nothing.

The morning after we first made love, waking up with my head on his chest, his heart beating under my ear.

The smile that lit his face when I surprised him at the hospital, bringing coffee and donuts for him and his staff.

The kiss that melted my bones, filled with tenderness and passion and a love so deep it stole my breath.

A sob catches in my throat. I can't do this. I can't give him up. Paul is my heart, my home, the best thing that's ever been mine.

How can I walk away from that? How can I leave behind the man who holds my soul in his hands?

I'm not strong enough. The thought of losing him crushes me into pieces too small to survive on my own.

But Paul's career is everything to him. He's worked and sacrificed for so long to achieve his dream, and I won't be the one to stand in his way. To drag him down.

He deserves so much more than that. So much more than *me*.

I have to give him up. No matter the cost. No matter if it breaks me.

For Paul, I would do anything. Even if it means letting go of the love that gave me wings.

The tears fall faster now, a deluge I'm powerless to stop. But underneath the heartbreak and sorrow, a flicker of peace ignites.

Because this is right. This is love—sacrificing for the good of the other person. Putting their needs first.

And Paul's needs come before my own. Always.

I take a deep, steadying breath and wipe my face. My heart may shatter into a thousand pieces, but I'll be damned if I don't do this with grace.

Paul deserves nothing less. Our love deserves nothing less.

It's time to say goodbye.

———

I stand outside Paul's door, every nerve in my body on fire. This is going to be the hardest thing I've ever done. But I have to stay strong. For Paul.

With a shaking hand, I knock twice. The door swings open immediately, and there he is—disheveled hair, tired eyes, and a smile that brightens my whole world.

"Britney." My name is a caress on his lips. "I've been waiting for you."

He pulls me into his arms, and I breathe him in for the last time. The scent of coffee and cologne that means home.

I cling to him, tears spilling onto his shirt. "Paul, we can't do this anymore."

He goes rigid against me. Pulls back with a frown. "What are you talking about?"

"Your reputation—" I break off with a sob. "I won't be the one to ruin your career. You've worked too hard for too long. You deserve so much more than a secret relationship."

"Britney, stop." His voice hardens. "I don't give a damn about my reputation. I care about you. Only you."

"But you should," I whisper. "You're an amazing doctor. You help people every single day. You can't throw that all away for me."

"I'm not throwing anything away. I want *you*, Britney. Only you." He cups my face, forcing me to meet his eyes. They shine with tears he refuses to shed. "We'll find a way to make this work. We belong together, and nothing is going to change that. Not my job, not the hospital, not anyone."

"Paul, please understand." I cling to his wrists, willing him to hear me. "I'm doing this for your own good. For the sake of your future."

"My future is with you." His voice breaks on the last word, and then he gets a crazed look in his eyes. "Britney, don't do this. Stay with me. We can get through anything as long as we're together. Haven't I taken care of you? I got you an apartment, a safe place to stay. I eliminated your monster."

My brow furrows. "Eliminated my monster?" Then my eyes widen as comprehension dawns on me. I cover my mouth with my hand to stifle my gasp. "Paul, please tell me you didn't do what I think you do."

Paul pulls me painfully close, wrapping his arms tight around me. "I did, Britney. I killed the scumbug who hurt you. I did it for you. To make sure he'll never hurt you again. No one will ever hurt you again. I can't stand that you've been crying all night."

Shock is still roiling through me when I register the last part of what he said. "How do you know I've been crying all night?"

Paul goes silent, but he doesn't release me.

"Paul?" I prompt him by pushing away from him—hard.

"I've been watching you all this time, Britney. I'm sorry. I know it's an invasion of your privacy, but I'm fucking obsessed with you." He spears his fingers through his hair, his eyes manic. "I can't live without you, Britney."

My face colors when I think of Paul watching me all this time when I thought I was alone. I'm still reeling from the knowledge that he murdered my stepdad too. Granted, there's no love lost between me and my stepdad. I'm not sad he's dead.

No, I'm sad that I drove Paul—a good, decent man —to this point. He killed because of *me*.

My stepdad was right. I taint everything I touch. I am my mother's daughter.

A good for nothing whore.

With a sob, I turn on my heels and run before Paul can stop me.

The last thing I hear is Paul calling out my name, pleading and heartbroken. I clench my jaw to hold in the sob rising in my throat. If I look back now, I will never have the strength to keep running.

So I keep my gaze forward and my feet moving, despite the ache in my chest so fierce I can barely breathe. Despite the voice in my head screaming that I'm making a mistake.

This is the only way. The only choice I have.

Paul continues to shout for me even as I exit the building and step out into the dim light of dusk. His cries echo in my mind, a desperate refrain I know will haunt me for the rest of my days.

But I harden my heart and keep walking down the lonely street, the taste of his last kiss lingering on my lips. The tears fall unheeded down my cheeks, dripping to the cracked pavement below.

With each step, I say a silent goodbye to the love I know I will never find again. To the man who holds my heart, even in our parting. Becaue despite everything, I don't care that he's a murderer now. I don't care that I turned him into a stalker. Because Paul is the only one I will ever want, now and forever, and he's lost to me.

CHAPTER
NINE

Paul

The walls close in around me as I lie awake, staring into the darkness. The sheets are cold without her warmth beside me.

Britney's scent lingers on the pillow, a haunting reminder of what I've lost.

I can't sleep. Can't eat. Can't breathe.

The days pass in a haze. At the hospital, I go through the motions, my mind far away from the patients who need me.

All I see is her face. All I hear is her laugh. We had something rare, something pure and true, and I let it slip through my fingers.

When I'm not at the hospital, I watch her apartment

from my car, waiting for a glimpse of her through the grimy windows. She lives in squalor now, alone and vulnerable. It's no surprise she didn't keep the luxurious apartment I secured for her. How could she after I confessed to watching her in it?

The thought of her in danger, hurting, tears me apart inside. I can't lose her.

I take a leave of absence from work. I have to make this right. Have to get her back where she belongs.

With me.

Always with me.

I pull up outside her apartment under cover of darkness. The neighborhood is quiet for once, the usual sounds of sirens and shouting muted in the dead of night.

The light in her window flickers out. She's alone.

It's time.

My knuckles rap against the rotting wooden door. Once. Twice.

When she opens the door, I'm struck breathless at the sight of her. Messy blonde hair falling around her shoulders. Gray eyes peering up at me through a fringe of lashes.

I was wrong to ever let her go.

She's *mine*. She's always been mine.

And I won't make the mistake of losing her again.

Britney's eyes widen, pupils dilating in the dim light of the hallway. "Paul? What are you doing here?"

Her words come out slurred, the scent of alcohol heavy on her breath. She sways unsteadily in the doorway, barely dressed in a thin camisole and panties.

Rage boils in my veins at the thought of her like this, vulnerable and exposed. But I swallow down the anger, forcing a smile. "I was worried about you."

"You shouldn't be here." She shakes her head, taking a stumbling step back. "We're not together anymore. You can't just show up whenever you want."

"I know, baby. I'm sorry, but you shouldn't be drinking. You're too young to drink, and you shouldn't do it like this anyway. Where did you even get alcohol, honey?" I reach out, grasping her upper arm as she loses her balance.

"My neighbor...she gets it for me," Britney hiccups, and my grip tightens, fingers pressing into the soft flesh of her arm. "I couldn't stay away, Britney. I had to make sure you were safe. Here. Let me help you."

She tries to pull away, but I don't release her. "Please, Paul. Just go." Tears shimmer in her eyes, and a sob catches in her throat.

The broken look on her face shreds me to pieces inside. I never meant to hurt her. I was only trying to protect her, to give her a good life.

"I'm so sorry," I whisper, drawing her into my arms.

She resists for a moment before collapsing against me, her body wracked with sobs. "It's going to be okay now. I'm here."

She suddenly pulls back from me and tries to turn away, but she wobbles and falls, crying out in pain as her ankle twists. Her eyes fly open, gaze sharpening with panic. "My ankle!" she whimpers. "I think I twisted it."

"I got you, baby," I try to soothe her as I scoop her up into my arms.

I don't know if she hears me or not because she promptly passes out in my arms—the side effect of too much alcohol, no doubt.

But she'll be okay. I'll make sure of it. I'm going to take care of her from now on whether she wants me to or not.

Britney's eyes flutter open as I carry her up the stairs to my apartment. "Where are we going?" she mumbles, words slurred with sleep and alcohol.

"Shh, it's okay." I brush a kiss against her forehead. "I'm taking you home."

"I hurt, Paul," she whimpers.

"I'm so sorry, baby." Guilt washes over me in a sickening wave. I never should have let her out of my sight. "Don't worry. I'll take care of you."

She blinks up at me, pale and trembling in my

arms. But she doesn't argue as I carry her down the hall. She knows she's safe with me now.

I lay Britney down on my bed, propping her foot up on a pillow. The ankle already looks swollen, purpling beneath her skin.

Kneeling beside her, I take her hand in mine. "I'm going to fix this, okay? I'll wrap your ankle and get you some ice and painkillers. And I'm going to stay here with you."

Britney's eyes widen. "You can't do that. People are counting on you at the hospital."

"You're all that matters to me." I squeeze her hand, willing her to understand. "My career means nothing if I can't have you. I haven't gone to work in a couple of weeks now."

She gasps. "Why?"

"How could I? When all I could do was obsess over you? I've been watching you this whole time, Britney, until I couldn't take it anymore. We belong together, baby. You must know that. You didn't make me quit my job. I don't want it without you. All I want is *you*. You've got to understand that, honey."

A war of emotions crosses her face, torn between longing and fear. But in the end, she looks away. Not yet ready to admit she feels the same way.

It doesn't matter. I can be patient. I've already lost

her once—I won't make that mistake again. This time, I'm playing for keeps.

I cup her cheek, turning her face back to mine. "Talk to me. Tell me you don't feel the same. I can't promise I'll leave you alone because God help me, Britney, you're under my skin. You're all I fucking think about, but tell me you don't still love me."

Her lips part, but no words come out. She can't say it. Won't say it.

"Britney." My thumb brushes over her soft skin. "Look at me."

When her eyes meet mine again, the truth is written there plain as day. She loves me as desperately as I love her.

"We belong together," I tell her softly. "No matter what anyone says, this is right. You're mine, Britney, just as I'm yours. We're meant to be together."

A tear slips down her cheek and I kiss it away. "I'm sorry," she whispers. "I'm so sorry I left you."

Joy and relief flood through me. "Shh, it's okay now. We're together again and that's all that matters. I'm never letting you go, Britney. Never again."

I cradle her face in my hands, our foreheads touching. So close I can feel her breath on my lips. But still my chest is tight. I need reassurance that she won't try to leave again. "Promise me. Promise you'll stay with me always."

She hesitates for only a moment before nodding. "I promise. I'm yours, Paul, forever."

Our lips meet then, sealing her promise with a kiss. The sweetness of her mouth, the warmth of her body in my arms again—it's like coming home.

We belong here, *together*. And this time, nothing will ever tear us apart.

EPILOGUE

Britney

One Year Later

PAUL'S clinic gleams under the fluorescent lights, a vision of sterility and precision. Everything in its place, orderly and controlled. Just like Paul.

He leads me through the front entrance, his hand resting on the small of my back, warmth seeping through the thin fabric of my blouse. "What do you think?"

I swallow hard, blinking at the sharp angles and reflective surfaces surrounding me. It's impressive. Meticulous. "It's very modern."

"Only the best for my patients." His eyes shine, lingering on my face. "I want them to know they're in capable hands."

My classes start next week, a new chapter waiting to unfold. But right now, all I can think about are Paul's hands—strong, confident hands that know exactly what they're doing. Hands that have touched every inch of my body, teasing and tormenting until I'm begging for release.

Paul crowds me against the reception desk, his breath hot against my ear. "I have an hour before my next patient arrives. Plenty of time to continue your...treatment."

Heat pools between my legs, my traitorous body responding to his proximity. I know I should refuse, keep our relationship professional, but the desire is too much. It always is with him. "I'm not sure that's appropriate." My protest lacks conviction.

A low chuckle. "When have we ever cared about appropriate?" His fingers skim the edge of my skirt, inching higher. "You're the one who wanted a more...hands-on approach to your therapy."

"Paul..." His name comes out as a moan as he finds the apex of my thighs. I love these games we play.

"That's Dr. Jameson to you." His eyes gleam with wicked intent. "Now, shall we begin your session? I think it's time to explore some new techniques."

Sharp desire spikes through me, melting away any lingering doubts. My addiction to this man will be my undoing, but I can't bring myself to care. Not when being with him feels so damn good.

I meet his smoldering gaze, a flush creeping into my cheeks. But my voice comes out steady, laced with challenge. "Do your worst, Doctor."

A wolfish grin. "With pleasure."

Then his mouth crashes into mine, and I surrender myself to his skillful hands once more.

Our passion burns white-hot, fueled by our ever-raging desire for one another that only seems to burn brighter every day. Paul's hands roam my body, setting my nerves aflame. I arch into him, craving the delicious friction of skin on skin.

"I need you," he murmurs against my throat, his lips and teeth scraping over my pulse point.

A groan escapes me as he grinds his hips into mine. "Then take me."

The blunt command spurs him into action. Clothing is shed in a flurry of movement, tossed haphazardly onto the floor.

Paul lifts me onto the counter, the granite cool against my heated skin. I wrap my legs around his waist, drawing him close. Our lips meet in a searing kiss, all teeth and tongue.

With a low, primal growl that resonates deep within

him, he slides into me. The sudden, fulfilling intrusion of him steals my breath away, leaving me gasping for more. His masculine scent fills my senses, mingling intoxicatingly with the musky aroma of our shared desire. I cling to him, my nails digging into the firmness of his back, overwhelmed by the intensity of the sensation that courses through me like electric current.

His body is chiseled; hard in all the right places and softer where it counts. His movements are powerful yet gentle, every action marked by a control that drives me wild with anticipation. My fingers explore, tracing the roadmap of muscles under his skin. His touch is hot against my skin, as though his very essence sparks with searing heat.

Our bodies intertwine. His mouths finds my neck, his warm breath sending shivers down my spine as he explores every inch of me. Our eyes lock, and in them I see a mirror of my own desire reflected back at me.

My body responds with equal fervor, fitting perfectly against him like two pieces of a lust-filled puzzle. Each arching movement hits a spot deep inside me that makes my toes curl in exquisite pleasure.

We're beyond words now. Only gasps and groans fill the room as we succumb to our primal urges, giving and taking in equal measure. Nothing else matters but this moment, this timeless dance of passion and desire that eclipses everything else.

He sets a punishing pace, his thrusts deep and hard. I meet each one, craving the exquisite pleasure-pain that sparks through my veins. The world narrows to this moment, this connection between us. Nothing else matters but the slide of skin, the meeting of bodies, the rhythmic beat of our hearts keeping time.

"Shit," he growls against my skin, pulling me closer to him as though we could somehow melt into one another. The feel of him buried deep inside me sends delicious shockwaves coursing through my veins as we reach that dizzying pinnacle—together.

And then Paul shifts, hitting a new angle that sends stars exploding behind my eyelids. A scream rises in my throat as my release crashes over me, wave after wave of ecstasy stealing my senses.

Through the haze of my climax, I'm dimly aware of Paul following after me, his hoarse shout echoing in my ears. We collapse against each other, a tangle of sated limbs and racing pulses.

In the aftermath, a bone-deep contentment suffuses me. Here, in Paul's arms, I've found my sanctuary. Here, I'm home.

We lie there for a long moment, catching our breath. Paul brushes a kiss against my temple, his hands tracing lazy circles on my back.

I nuzzle into his neck, inhaling his scent. "I love

you." The words slip out without conscious thought, a simple truth.

His arms tighten around me. "I love you too, Britney. So much."

A lump forms in my throat at the raw emotion in his voice. Here, in the warmth of Paul's embrace, I've finally found my home. My heart swells with joy and gratitude, overflowing with love for this man who has healed my wounds and made me whole again.

I nestle closer to my husband, draping my leg over his. Our bodies fit together perfectly, two pieces of the same whole.

"You're thinking deep thoughts," he murmurs against my hair.

"Just feeling grateful." I tilt my head up, seeking his lips. The kiss is slow and sweet, unhurried.

He pulls back, gazing into my eyes. "I never thought I could be this happy." His thumb traces the line of my jaw, rough and calloused from years of medical practice. "You've changed everything, Britney. Brought light to my darkness."

"You saved me," I whisper. "In so many ways, you saved me."

His eyes soften with emotion as he cups my face in his hands. "And you saved me right back."

I lean in, capturing his mouth again. The kiss deepens, igniting the embers of desire within me. My hands roam over his chest and shoulders, reveling in the feel of his skin under my palms.

Paul rolls onto his back, pulling me on top of him. I straddle his hips, grinding against him as our tongues dance. Heat pools between my legs, an aching need for him to fill me once more.

His hands grip my waist, guiding my movements. "I can never get enough of you." His voice is rough with want. "No one has ever made me feel the way you do."

I rock against him, craving the delicious friction. "Paul..." My plea hangs in the air, laced with longing.

He lifts his hips, pressing against me. I moan at the contact, awash in sensation. "What is it, baby? What do you need?"

I gaze down at him through half-lidded eyes, seeing the love and desire reflected in his own. "You. I just need you."

A smile tugs at his lips as his hands slide up to cup my breasts. "Then take me, Britney. I'm yours."

And so I do. Again and again, losing myself in his embrace. Here, in this place beyond words, we find a profound connection that transcends the physical. Two souls and bodies intertwined, moving as one.

This is bliss.

This is home.

Want a free Emma Bray book? Go to www. authoremmabray.com!

www.ingramcontent.com/pod-product-compliance
Lightning Source LLC
Chambersburg PA
CBHW061438160726
47995CB00003B/952